Elemental Love

Written & illustrated by

Janet Crosby

ISBN 978-1-7389406-0-8
Library and Archives Canada
03/16/2023

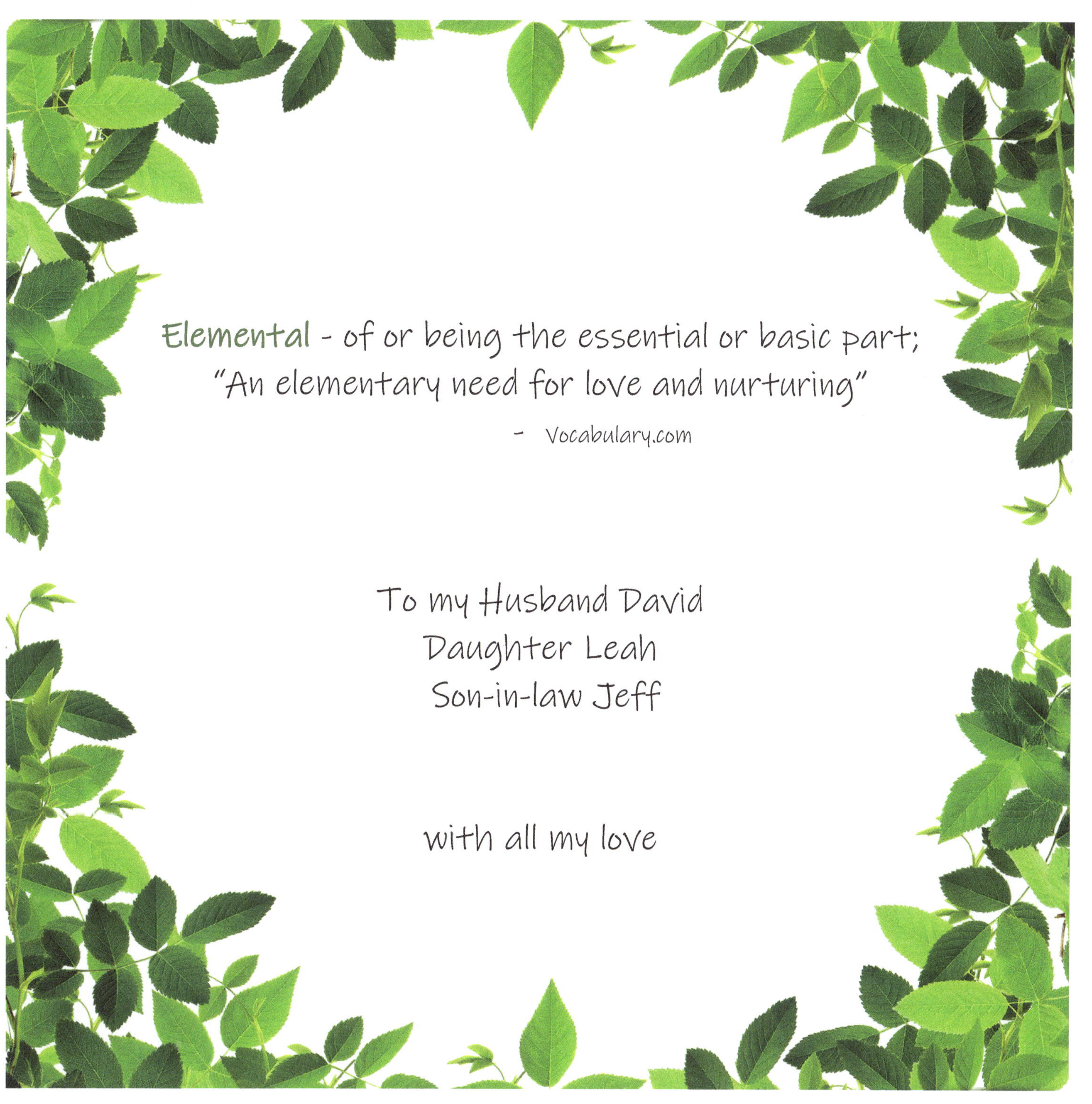

Elemental - of or being the essential or basic part;
"An elementary need for love and nurturing"
– Vocabulary.com

To my Husband David
Daughter Leah
Son-in-law Jeff

with all my love

Elemental Love Contents

Introducing the Elementals

Elementals are associated with a particular element of nature

such as earth, wind, water or fire.

The Elementals in this story book are Fairies, Elves, Dwarfs and Gnomes.

They are associated with the element of earth.

They are also known as the wee folk.

Fairies have wings and can be both male & female. Some have snouts.

Elves are tall, slim, usually attractive, with very large ears.

Dwarfs are short and stocky.

Gnomes are tiny and thin, with very long noses.

The Yellow-Green Hills
Janet Crosby

The Yellow-Green Hills

Across the majestic high mountain peaks,
Along the meandering rivers and creeks.

Into the deep, dark forest of trees,
Making our way through miles of leaves.

Behind the waterfall crystal and blue,
Soft, rolling hills come into view.

The sky will be bright, the hills yellow-green,
The loveliest place you've ever seen.

Many a wee folk have gathered there,
Enjoying each other and the weather so fair.

Meet Delmar, the tiny dwarf; he's a bit shy,
Turning away, not meeting your eye.

Penston Gnome is a talkative sort,
Spinning his tales, he doesn't keep short.

You may try to deter him, to no avail,
As he loves the attention in tall hat and coattail.

Many dwarfs are about simply having a chat,
Each wearing a very tall, colorful hat.

There is red, purple, green on many a fellow,
While others are wearing orange, blue and yellow.

Two lovely, tall elves are strolling on by,
Smiling at tiny dwarfs sitting nearby,

Who are chatting, laughing and being at play,
Simply enjoying the beautiful day!

Frileena Fairy

Frileena Fairy

Frileena the fairy was sad as could be
And had flown to the branch of a very high tree.

All Elementals had come out to see
Why Frileena was weeping high up in that tree.

Duffington Dwarf tried to help her along
Saying, "Won't you come down and tell us what's wrong?"

"Well, my hair is not cool like Bruweena's," she said.
"Mine simply lies there, flat on my head."

Bruweena, the elf child, was lovelier than most,
With a sweet disposition, not given to boast.

Ah ha!", said the mayor in his orange and blue coat.
"This is simply a matter of envy, let's note.

Sweet little Frileena, you're able to fly
High up above us you flit in the sky.

Look within, your own special gifts you'll discover,
Never comparing yourself to another.

Then you'll be happy and much more content.
Wouldn't this time be much better spent?"

<u>An Elemental Reflection</u>

We are all different and unique. You will fly,
too, once you discover the special gifts you
were born with and use them to
create the life you desire.

Derek the Dwarf
Janet Crosby

Derek the Dwarf

Derek the dwarf was not like the rest;
He looked more like a bear in trousers and vest.

Senora, the snout fairy, she understood
As snouts were not always accepted as good.

Both knew they looked different, this was a fact,
But inside, their elementalism was just as intact.

Their awesome uniqueness made them best of friends,
Enjoying the good vibes acceptance extends.

Then, one fine day, Knuckles the gnome climbed a tree,
Fell from a high place and injured his knee.

Derek the dwarf did come right away,
To see if Gnome Knuckles would be okay.

Taking one look, Knuckles' knee did he pop,
Back into place with a skip and a hop.

A natural healer was Derek, you see,
He was giving and loving and kind to a tee.

All could see then, he was more than his face,
He was caring and gentle with God-given grace.

With their love, Derek did blossom and grow.
The wee folk were happy, too, don't we reap what we sow?

<u>An Elemental Reflection</u>

An individual is more than their outer
appearance. To really see them,
aspire to know them on the inside.

Grandfather Nicholas Gnome
Janet Crosby

Grandfather Nicholas Gnome

Grandfather Nicholas Gnome
Had a very lovely creek-side home.

Many an hour he would spend,
Fishing chub in the deep creek's bend.

The elementals gathered there,
To swim and bathe and wash their hair.

When his grandson came to stay,
Nicholas took him there to play.

Timothy Gnome was inches tall,
So, his voice didn't carry far at all.

Timothy Gnome was always talking,
Sitting, standing, eating, walking.

Nicholas, with his hearing gone,
Couldn't take this for very long.

He would have to strain to listen,
Still, parts of words he'd still be missin'.

Many questions came from Tim,
His mind being full right to its brim.

What's that floating in the water?
Is that a furry baby otter?

Why are those mountains so very pink?
If I fell in, do you think I'd sink?

Why does that cloud look just like a dog?
What's sitting over there on that log?

Why do these insects fly in my face?
Why're these rocks all here in one place?

What is that bird singing up in that tree?
Do you think he is talking to you and to me?

Grandfather, why am I so much smaller
Then everyone else who's so much taller?

On and on till the end of the day,
when Nicholas Gnome would lovingly say,

"Timothy, my sweet little chap,
I think we are both in much need of a nap."

So then, grandfather Nicholas Gnome,
Would carry tiny Timothy Gnome home.

<u>An Elemental Reflection</u>

Patience is a very nice way of demonstrating love.

Farrington Fairy
Janet Crosby

Farrington Fairy

One very balmy summer's day,
Farrington Fairy went out to play.

He flew and flew too far from home,
Suddenly finding himself lost and alone.

He needed some help, this much was true,
But, who to ask, he hadn't a clue?

Then seeing wee folk down below,
He flew on down to say hello!

He asked them if they'd be so kind,
His way back home for him to find.

Cause to Farrington, it wasn't clear,
How to make his way to there from here.

Happily, some elves did know,
Exactly the way he'd have to go.

Elf father and son, they had a talk,
Discussing the way, he'd have to walk.

They said to head directly south,
Turn due left at the river's mouth.

"Please move quickly past little homes,
Of the tiny, skinny, long nosed-gnomes.

Past the bog and please be perky,
As the water's green and kinda murky.

Careful through the winding hollow,
If you get lost, just ask the swallow.

Over the hill that's steep and narrow,
Across the fields the farmers' farrowed.

Watch the scarecrow on the right,
He may give you quite a fright!

Into the tunnel dark, please hurry,
You'll be fine, try not to worry.

Exit onto the fairy slope,
This should see you home, we hope."

Trying his hardest not to cry,
Farrington Fairy said, "Oh, my!

This whole ordeal has been most stressing.
The journey home too much, I'm guessing.

Think I'd rather let it be,
Knowing mom will come for me."

<u>An Elemental Reflection</u>

Always rely on your own good judgement.

Janet Crosby

Dwarf Dwiggins's Wisdom Word

All the wee folk, they had heard
About Dwarf Dwiggins's wisdom word.

Those who found him on their searches,
Said he lives among the birches.

On flat rocks he makes his home.
His wisdom desk is made of stone.

The wee folk waiting at this spot,
I'm told amount to quite a lot.

They've also said that I should know,
Dwarf Dwiggins puts on quite a show.

His hat grows very tall, it's said,
Rising high above his head.

And that the new created space is
Full of many spirit faces.

This you may find very vexing,
Thinking with your mind I'm messing.

If so, I am truly sorry,
I only pass along the story.

Then Dwiggins does his message tell,
As if he's under some deep spell.

"I clearly hear from up above,
The word to share with you is LOVE.

Also, in this book it's written,
And confirmed by Wisdom Kitten."

What he continued on to say,
Remains with me this very day.

"Kindness, thoughtfulness, compassion,
Be as one, make this the fashion.

Gnome and Dwarf, Elf and Fairy,
Having fun and making merry.

What's most important, twixt you and me?
It's elemental love you see!"

An Elemental Reflection

But the greatest of these is love.

Balork

Balork

Far off, near limestone mountain ridges,
where steep rock and forest bridges,

Deep trails wind through ancient trees,
Leaves sing happily in the breeze.

By a gentle, moving stream,
Lies a village, lush and green.

Right there at the water's fork,
Lives an elf boy, named Balork.

Balork, he loves to go explore,
His parents' warnings to ignore.

Off he goes most every day,
To roam, to laugh, to be at play.

You'll find him by the water blue,
Catching him a frog or two.

Poking sticks into some holes,
Along the mud walls, as he goes.

Out fly hornets, "Ouch! One stung me!
Off I go, I'll climb that tall tree.

There's a nest of baby birds,
They're so cute, I have no words.

I'll take one home, such a nice pet,
Hope my parents aren't too upset."

Walking through tall golden grasses,
Beautiful wildflowers all in masses.

Finding garter snakes to keep,
In his pockets they can sleep.

Heading up this mountain pathway,
Kinda steep, "Awe, I'll be okay.

Looking down's a little scary,
Is it safe to eat this berry?

There's a cave, a place where things hide,
I'll just take a look, what's inside?"

And what did young Balork discover?
Stick-plumed birds and their mother.

The birds, the village tales he'd been told,
They are worth their weight in pure gold!

They're thought to bring hope, change and
freedom,
Everyone will want to see them.

After, he was quite the hero,
His status going to ten from zero.

Balork would stand there, simply smiling,
Truthfully, a bit beguiling.

His huge eyes wide and all a-glitter,
Each pocket home to some small critter.

<u>An Elemental Reflection</u>

Be adventurous.
Don't be afraid to take a risk, because it's through discovery,
that we learn about the world and ourselves.